GILBERTO AND THE WIND

Also by Marie Hall Ets

In the Forest
Play with Me
Just Me
Elephant in a Well

By Marie Hall Ets and Aurora Labastida

Nine Days to Christmas

BY MARIE HALL ETS

GILBERTO

I am *Gilberto*
and this is the story
of me and the Wind

AND THE WIND

THE VIKING PRESS • NEW YORK

My thanks to Gilberto
and his mother — and
to Pepe, too — for helping
me make this book

VIKING KESTREL
Viking Penguin Inc., 40 West 23rd Street, New York, New York 10010, U.S.A.
Penguin Books Ltd, 27 Wrights Lane, London W8 5TZ (Publishing & Editorial) and
Harmondsworth, Middlesex, England (Distribution & Warehouse)
Penguin Books Australia Ltd, Ringwood, Victoria, Australia
Penguin Books Canada Limited, 2801 John Street, Markham, Ontario, Canada L3R 1B4
Penguin Books (N.Z.) Ltd, 182–190 Wairau Road, Auckland 10, New Zealand

Copyright © Mary Hall Ets, 1963
All rights reserved
First published in 1963 by Viking Penguin Inc.
Published simultaneously in Canada
Printed in the United States of America

13   15   17   19   20   18   16   14   12
Library of Congress catalog card number: 63-8527
ISBN 0-670-34025-1

I hear Wind whispering at the door. "You-ou-ou," he whispers. "You-ou-ou-ou!" So I get my balloon, and I run out to play.

5

At first Wind is gentle and just floats my balloon around in the air.

But then, with a jerk, he grabs it away and carries it up to the top

6

of a tree. "Wind! Oh, Wind!" I say. "Blow it back to me! *Please!*"
But he won't. He just laughs and whispers,*"You-ou-ou-ou!"*

7

Wind loves to play with the wash on the line. He blows the pillow slips into balloons and shakes the sheets and twists the apron strings.

8

And he pulls out all the clothespins that he can. Then he tries on
the clothes—though he knows they're too small.

9

And Wind loves umbrellas. Once when I took one out in the rain

10

he tried to take it away from me. And when he couldn't, he broke it.

If the gate in the pasture is left unlatched, Wind plays with that, too.
He opens it up, then bangs it shut, making it squeak and cry.

"Wind! Oh, Wind!" I say, and I go and climb on. "Give me a ride!"
But with me on it the gate is too heavy. Wind can't move it at all.

13

When the grass is tall in the meadow Wind and I like to race. Wind
runs ahead, then comes back and starts over. But he always wins,

14

because he just runs over the top of the grass and I have to run through it and touch the ground with my feet.

When the big boys on the hill have kites to fly Wind helps *them* out.
Wind carries *their* kites way up to the sky and all around.

But when *I* have a kite Wind won't fly it at all. He just drops it.

"Wind! Oh, Wind!" I say. "I don't like you today!"

When the apples are ripe in the fall, I run with Wind to the pasture and wait under the tree. And Wind always blows one down for me.

21

And when I have a boat with a paper sail Wind comes and sails it

22

for me — just as he sails *big* sailboats for sailors on the sea.

And when I have a pinwheel Wind comes and plays, too. First I
blow it myself to show him how. Then I hold it out, or hold it up,

24

and Wind blows it for me. And when he blows it, he turns it so fast
that it whistles and sings, and all I can see is a blur.

Wind likes my soap bubbles best of all. *He* can't make the bubbles
—*I* have to do that. But he carries them way up into the air for the

sun to color. Then he blows some back and makes me laugh when they burst in my eyes or on the back of my hand.

27

When the leaves have fallen off the trees I like to sweep them into
a pile. But then Wind comes along. And just to show that he can

28

sweep without a broom, Wind scatters the leaves all about again.
And he blows the dirt in my face.

29

Sometimes Wind is so strong he starts breaking the trees and
knocking down fences. Then I'm afraid. I run in the house and

lock the door. And when Wind comes howling after me and tries to squeeze in through the keyhole, I tell him, "No!"

31

But then comes a day when Wind is all tired out. "Wind," I whisper. "Oh, Wind! Where are you?" "Sh-sh-sh-sh," answers Wind, and he stirs one dry leaf to show where he is. So I lie down beside him and we both go to sleep — under the willow tree.